THE ADVENTURES OF "CHUCK E. BEAVER" AND FRIENDS

SUMMER CAMP

Written by
Kiki

Illustrated by
Robert Elliot

Published by
Montbec Inc.

Publisher
MATT ARENY

Publication Advisor
JOSE AZEVEDO

Editorial Supervisor
ETHEL SALTZMAN

Artwork Supervisor
PIERRE RENAUD

ISBN 2-89227-214-9

Chuck E.'s second year at school was ending and summer was fast approaching. Mr. and Mrs. Beaver had already talked to Chuck E. about going to summer camp for part of the summer. Many of Chuck E.'s friends would be there and there would be lots of new things Chuck E. would learn.

However, Chuck E. wasn't sure he wanted to go to camp. He knew he would be away from his mom and dad for two whole weeks and he had never done that before. Going to school for the first time had been frightening enough, but what would happen to him if he was away from home for two weeks?

"Chuck E., why don't you want to go to summer camp?" Mrs. Beaver asked.

"Oh, Mom, I don't know what it will be like being away from you, Pop, and the baby for so long," Chuck E. told her. "I would miss you all so much that I doubt if I would really enjoy myself."

"But, son, remember how you felt when you had to go to school for the first time," Mrs. Beaver pointed out. "You were also afraid then that you would miss us too much, but when you got there and realized all the fun you were having, you didn't want to leave."

"Summer camp will be the same, you'll see!" she continued. "All of your friends will be there and we'll call every day to see how you are!"

"Will you, Mom?" Chuck E. asked hopefully. "You were right about school, so maybe I should give summer camp a try. But you've got to promise to call every day because I'm going to miss you a lot!"

"I promise, son," Mrs. Beaver agreed as she hugged Chuck E. tight. It was now two weeks later and the school year was over. Summer camp at Lake Pow Pow was to begin in a week.

All of Chuck E.'s friends had been looking forward to getting back to summer camp, and their clothes were already packed. Camp Keechewawa was no more than an hour's drive from Little Forest. It was located on beautiful Lake Pow Pow which was named after a legendary Indian princess from the Keechewawa tribe who had lived there many years ago.

Part of the summer camp tradition was to have the children experience what life was like for the Keechewawa tribe. They would learn all about building fires, making teepees, canoeing and hiking in the woods.

The bus for Camp Keechewawa was to leave on Saturday morning. Chuck E. was busy packing when his father walked into his bedroom.

"Chuck E., can I give you a hand?" Mr. Beaver asked.

"I don't think so, Pop," Chuck E. replied. "I guess I'm going to have to learn to get used to doing things myself for the next two weeks."

"Well, I understand, son," Mr. Beaver said. "But don't be afraid to ask for help when you really need it, okay?"

"Okay, Pop, I promise," Chuck E. smiled.

"Just remember, son, summer camp with your friends will be a lot of fun." Mr. Beaver reassured Chuck E., "but we'll be right here in case you want to call anytime just to talk."

"Thanks, Pop!" Chuck E. said gratefully. "I just might do that!"

Soon it was Saturday and everyone was
at the bus station waiting to board the
bus to Camp Keechewawa. Gerty, Bobby,
Marty, Chippy, Skippy and Chuck E. were
all there along with many other children
and their parents.

18

"Say, Chuck E., is this your first time going to Camp Keechewawa?" Chippy asked.

"It is, Chippy," Chuck E. replied, "and I'm a little nervous about being away from home for so long."

"Oh, don't worry, Chuck E.," Gerty reassured him. "We were the same the first time we went to camp, but there was so much to do that we hardly missed home at all!"

"Gerty's right!" Marty added. "We learned so much that we were sad when we finally had to leave. I guess we get a little homesick once in a while but we all comfort one another so it isn't so bad."

"I'm so glad all of you will be there!"
Chuck E. told his friends. "At least you'll
help me get my mind off home."
"So, what exactly does everyone do at
camp?" Chuck E. asked curiously.

"Oh, there are so many things!"
Bobby answered. "There's hiking, sailing,
canoeing, bird-watching, campfires, sing-
a-longs, and best of all, lots of eating!"

"Oh boy!" Chuck E. shouted, "I can
hardly wait!"

Soon the bus was ready to leave, and the parents said goodbye. Chuck E. was one of the last children to board the bus.

"Goodbye, son," Mr. and Mrs. Beaver said lovingly as they kissed Chuck E. "Have a good time and remember to listen to your counsellor."

"I will," Chuck E. reassured them. "And don't forget to call!"

"We won't, son," Mr. Beaver promised as Chuck E. boarded the bus.

All of the children were in their seats with their backpacks tucked high above them. The bus driver closed the door and the bus started on its way to Camp Keechewawa.

The bus ride took about an hour, winding up into the mountains around Lake Pow Pow. As they got near the lake, Chuck E. looked out and saw Camp Keechewawa nestled on one side surrounded by large mountains.

"Boy, I didn't realize it was this beautiful up here!" Chuck E. commented.

"Wait till you see it at night under the stars around a campfire!" Bobby exclaimed. "That's when it's most beautiful!"

"Really!" Chuck E. remarked excitedly. "And look, we even have log cabins to sleep in!" he added as he pointed to the many cabins on the edge of the lake.

"'Oh, yeah, Chuck E.!" Bobby continued. "You're really going to like it here!"

"You know, Bobby," Chuck E. replied, "I think you're right!"

Soon the bus pulled to a stop in front of the main building of Camp Keechewawa. A tall man, dressed in traditional Indian clothing, appeared at the front door of the building with eight younger Indian braves. He was Mr. Grizzler, the camp's head counsellor, and the younger ones were the junior counsellors who were assigned to each cabin.

As everyone got off the bus they were greeted by Mr. Grizzler. They soon gathered in a large group in front of the main building.

"Good morning, girls and boys,"
Mr. Grizzler spoke loudly. "Welcome to
Camp Keechewawa! I will be your head
counsellor this year, and each cabin
group will also have its junior counsellor
who is one of the braves beside me. If
you would please find yourself a group of
six, then we can get you settled in your
cabins."

"Oh, boy, this means we can all be
together!" Chuck E. exclaimed. "Bobby,
Gerty, Marty, Chippy, Skippy and myself
makes six!"

"Sorry, Chuck E., I have to group with
the girls," Gerty announced. "But we'll
be seeing one another all of the time!"

"Oh, yeah, I forgot," Chuck E. said
disappointedly.

Gerty went off to join some of her girl friends while the rest of the gang stayed together. It turned out that there weren't enough children to get a sixth member for Chuck E.'s group, so they left it at five. The groups were each assigned a junior counsellor and they were soon off to their cabins. Each cabin had three double bunk beds and one washroom.

"Who's going to take the top bunk?" Chippy asked.

"Oh, I'm afraid of heights," Marty explained with some embarrassment. "Can I have the bottom, please?"

"Sure, Marty," Skippy replied, "I don't mind taking the top!"

"Neither do I," Chuck E. added, "but if you prefer the top, Chippy, you can have it."

"Well, I'm used to heights, Chuck E.," Chippy remarked, "so maybe it's best if I take it."

"Okay, I'm glad because I don't care much for heights either," Chuck E. admitted.

Soon everyone had their own beds and had put away their belongings. A loud bell was heard coming from outside and the gang's junior counsellor announced that lunch was ready.

They quickly followed their counsellor to the mess hall where the cook was serving lunch.

"Oh, boy! Food!" Chuck E. exclaimed with excitement.

Everyone was hungry after the long bus ride and they really enjoyed the hearty meal. After lunch each group was allowed to tour the camp facilities with their counsellor. Chuck E. was very impressed with everything from the boating facilities to the many hiking trails.

That night everyone gathered for a big
campfire by the lake where Mr. Grizzler
told them the story of the beautiful
Indian princess Pow Pow and the
Keechewawa tribe. Chuck E. was thrilled
by all of the stories and the beautiful fire.
It hadn't occurred to him that the day
was almost over and he hadn't missed his
parents at all.

Chuck E.'s parents did call that night to see how he was getting on, but Chuck E. wasn't missing home very much.

"Are you alright, son?" Mrs. Beaver asked with concern.

"Oh, I'm alright, Mom," Chuck E. replied happily. "It's been a wonderful day, and I can't wait to see what's going to happen tomorrow!"

"I'm so glad, son," Mrs. Beaver said joyfully. "I knew once you got there, things would work out just fine!"

"You were right, Mom!" Chuck E. agreed. "Call tomorrow so that I can tell you everything that happened, okay?"

"Alright, son," Mrs. Beaver agreed, "we'll do just that."

Over the next two weeks Chuck E. learned what it was like to be a brave in the Keechewawa tribe. He learned how to canoe, sail, build fires, make teepees and do many more things that the Keechewawas did long ago.

His mom and dad called every day and they were thrilled to talk to him. In fact, they missed Chuck E. much more than he missed them, but they were glad he was having such a good time. Chuck E. had made many new friends and discovered that summer camp was a wonderful experience after all. It was one that he would continue to enjoy for many summers to come.

Summer camp is a wonderful place

To do things to your liking.

You'll make new friends, and you'll learn

Sailing, swimming, and hiking!

Your friend,

Chuck E.